The Eye of Espinoza

TY SPENCER VOSSLER

This is a work of fiction. Names, characters, places, and incidents are products of the author's imagination or are used fictitiously and are not to be construed as real. Any resemblance to actual events, locations, organizations, or persons, living or dead, is entirely coincidental.

World Castle Publishing, LLC
Pensacola, Florida
Copyright © Ty Spencer Vossler 2017
Paperback ISBN: 9781629896717
eBook ISBN: 9781629896724
First Edition World Castle Publishing, LLC, April 24, 2017
http://www.worldcastlepublishing.com

Licensing Notes

Cover: Karen Fuller
Editor: Maxine Bringenberg

CHAPTER 1

On a cold, grey morning, December 1952, dim light filtered into the living rooms of two-story Victorian homes in Binghamton, New York. The naked branches of the tree-lined residential streets served as resting perches for families of crows, who laughed at the white, snow-covered world around them. Albert Schweitzer had just won the Nobel Peace Prize, Cheez Whiz was thrust upon innocent North American pallets, Joseph McCarthy ordered Charles Chaplin to get out of town, there were 58,000 cases of polio in the United States, and New York installed traffic lights. The word *smog* was coined in London.

"Jonathan, have you seen Mr. Espinoza lately?" inquired Emily Smythe as she peered out the kitchen window to the house next door.

A middle-aged man sitting in his favorite leather chair distractedly peered up from the morning newspaper. "No dear, I have not, and I can't say I'm disappointed."

"Odd, don't you think? He hasn't picked up his paper for over a week. They are scattered all over his front lawn."

Jonathan snapped the paper. "Maybe he's on vacation—Florida, if he's got any sense."

"You know that Mr. Espinoza doesn't go *anywhere*."

"True, he doesn't get out much," he sighed, trying to find where he had left off on the sports page.

She turned to look at her husband. "But

it is just strange. I usually see him coming to get his papers."

"Maybe he's shacked up with one of his whores." He hoped she would give it a rest so that he could get on with reading the news.

"Darling, Mr. Espinoza must be in his late seventies, early eighties," she muttered. "Highly unlikely."

Jonathan shook his paper and peered over the edge. "For all I care he's building a bomb shelter in his backyard."

"I think it's strange is all. He always comes for his paper like clockwork."

"Jesus...." Jonathan rolled his eyes. "If it's eating on you so much, go pay him a neighborly visit—just don't get too close."

***

Emily gazed into the swirling clouds of her coffee. "Perhaps I will," she announced stubbornly, and then took the bedroom stairs two at a time to change out of her flannel nightgown. Perhaps he'll ask to paint me, she imagined, and *this* time I'll say yes.

Jonathan was listening to a radio music show when Emily marched downstairs in a heavy sweater, green snowcap with earflaps, and a red scarf. Vera Lynn was crooning, "*Auf Wiedersehn, Sweetheart.*"

"I'll be right back," she announced as she tugged on her winter boots.

"Going to check on Picasso?" quipped her husband. "Hey, listen to this." He snapped the newspaper and pointed to an article. "Says here, Christine Jorgensen, a transsexual in Denmark, was the first recipient of a successful sexual reassignment operation. Can you imagine?"

Emily offered no comment as she slipped on her gloves.

He slapped the paper down in resignation. "Jeez, give me a second...I'll go with you." His knees popped as he lifted out of the chair. "Where are my boots?"

"In the mudroom where they always are." Emily waited patiently as he forced his feet into the snow boots.

"Christ, could they make these any harder to get on?"

If Jonathan only knew the truth about Mr. Espinoza, she smiled to herself. In years past Espinoza had undressed her with his eyes. It was a feeling she'd grown to enjoy, and what strange eyes they were. His clear blue one seemed kindly, yet the other was wild, murky, and incapable of perceiving anything but shadows.

In fifteen years her chance meetings with Mr. Espinoza had invariably been pleasant. She met him walking in the park, the local grocery store, and at the community mailbox, where he once surprised her with a query, delivered in an exotic Spanish accent. "Ah,

Mrs. Smythe, you look lovely today. Would you consider allowing me to paint you?" His words tickled her ear. "Such beauty as you possess should be immortalized."

Emily blushed, demurred, and secreted the inquiry deep inside her heart—too precious to share, especially with Jonathan. All those years ago he had greeted her with his kind eye, and yet how she had yearned to know what he was thinking behind the other one. She would return his consideration now by showing her neighborly concern.

CHAPTER 2

"*Temptation*," by Mario Lanza, hung in the bitter air as they trudged through the squeaking snow to Mr. Espinoza's house. When they arrived, her husband assumed command. He knocked forcefully, and absently stooped down for a moist newspaper that had reached the porch.

"Damned paperboy couldn't hit the broad side of a barn," Jonathan complained. Although he grumbled about Espinoza, he was more curious than Emily. He had seen several Espinoza paintings hanging above the bar at Paddy's Pub. One depicted a couple rollicking naked among steaming forest leaves, and the other depicted an orgy on the beach, seagulls gliding above. Paddy, whose Irish accent thickened when he gossiped, explained, "Espinoza tol' me once that his paintin' shows nature in its purest form. Know what I says back?" He pointed to one particularly impressive woman spread out on a sand dune. "I says to 'im, I wouldn't mind doin' what comes natural with the likes'a her."

A chorus of laughter rose in the bar and then died like the end of a belch.

"Christ," Jonathan mumbled, knocking louder. "Mr. Espinoza, it's the Smythes from next door!

"Mr. Espinoza!" Emily joined.

Jonathan tried peeking through the front curtains, then he stepped off the porch to stare up at the large upstairs windows. He thought he detected movement there. Emily tried the door and it opened with an alarming series of screeches and squawks.

"Have you gone mad? You can't just waltz into a man's—"

***

"Mr. Espinoza? It's Mrs. Smythe, are you home?" The sparsely furnished living area nearly swallowed her inquiry.

"God almighty, it stinks in here." Jonathan covered his nose with a sleeve and swatted flies. "This must be where the flies hunker down for winter."

"Something's not right." Her eyes darted around the room.

Jonathan didn't answer, yet shared the feeling. He startled Emily by touching her arm. "We should call the police," he suggested.

"Cat pee," she answered. "Do you smell it?"

On cue, a thin yellow cat ran in from the kitchen yowling and rubbing frantically against Emily's legs. "Poor thing's starving." The cat used her leg as a scratching post, and she gently pushed it off.

They went into the kitchen, where the cat had licked piles of dirty dishes clean and shattered several in the act. An open space next to the small dining table had doubled as a cat box. Emily rummaged through the cupboards for anything the cat could eat. The refrigerator was bare except for two bottles of Pabst beer and a few dried out cartons of Chinese take-out.

"Darling, would you fetch some tuna from the pantry?" Emily used endearments with good effect whenever she needed something done.

The desperate cat continued to yowl, insinuating itself between her ankles and nipping at them. She noticed that it was missing part of an ear and sported a crooked tail.

Jonathan gave a Nazi salute. "*Ya vol, frau* Smythe," and then brushed a fly away from his mouth.

Emily smiled, adding, "And you should call the police just to be on the safe side."

He clicked his heels together, spun a one-eighty, and strolled out.

The cat was intractable. Emily cooed, "Where's your friend, huh?"

"Yow-yow-yow!" it answered.

Emily opened the kitchen window to let flies escape and returned to the living area, anxious for her husband's return.

Strange, she thought, for an artist not to display his work. The walls were vacant, although she saw rectangles and squares where paintings had once hung. Warily she walked to the stairwell. She remembered the layout of the house from when it had belonged to the Worthingtons, fifteen years before. The bedrooms were up there. Flies crisscrossed in her path as she ascended.

"Mr. Espinoza, it's Mrs. Smythe." The creaking stairs made her uneasy. In her house, she could always pinpoint Jonathan's location by the floorboards. "Mr. Espinoza?"

The two smaller side bedrooms were open and empty. *He's moved out,* she thought. Straight ahead was the master suite.

The cat weaved between her ankles and she nudged it aside. It protested and returned instantly. Emily knocked on the door. "Señor Espinoza?"

She put an ear to the door, opened just a crack to peek in. Droning flies covered the two large windows facing the street, allowing in a staccato of dim morning light as they shifted around. Overwhelmed by the stench, she summoned her courage, took a deep breath, and stepped inside.

"Mister—"

As she turned her head to the right, a

scream lodged in her throat. She backed out of the room, sank to her knees, and vomited through the stair rail. The cat scampered down the stairs to lap up the remnants of Mrs. Smythe's breakfast.

CHAPTER 3

"The men in blue are on their way!" Jonathan announced from the doorway, and then heard his wife's gasping sobs. He climbed the stairs two at a time and kneeled to take her in his arms. "Darling, are you all right?"

The smell punched his nose and flies darted everywhere, buzzed in his hair, trying to access his nose, eyes, and mouth. He tugged Emily to her feet and she pointed to the bedroom.

"Yes, dear, I can imagine," he managed to say. He hurried her out of the house and sat her on the front porch. Then he put

17

a handkerchief to his nose. "I'll be right back...the police are on the way."

"Jonathan please, don't go in there — horrible — dreadful."

"I'll just be a moment, I promise." He inhaled deeply and ran up the stairs. Taking another deep breath, he stepped into Espinoza's bedroom.

"Sweet mother of — "

Mr. Espinoza lay in bed, his skeletal arms extended into a cross from his bloated body. The mouth was open, and the wriggling offspring of flies thrived there. Espinoza's shadow eye was open, fixed on the ceiling, and the clear one was closed in a sardonic wink. The cat leaped to the bed to see what could be had. With a reflective bite, it snatched a fly in mid-air and chewed.

Jonathan staggered out and led Emily to the front steps of their home until police arrived. Emily quivered in his arms. He held her tightly as police entered and opened the windows of the house. The flies were in no hurry to leave their cozy paradise. A stiff breeze sifted through the grisly scene and carried the smell for an instant.

"Fuck," Jonathan whispered to himself.

She looked up at her husband and her eyes narrowed. "Did you just say what I think you said?"

"No," he countered.

"I distinctly heard you."

"The fuck you did."

Emily burst out laughing. He rose to his feet, reached for his wife, and guided her inside with one arm hooked under her armpit. He loved her dearly at that moment. As they arrived at the safety of their kitchen, the police arrived and Jonathan guided them to Mr. Espinoza's front door. A light wind had begun to blow as he returned to his wife.

They heard the movement of feet, tramping up stairs, opening and closing doors. Then they heard a door close with a loud bang, followed closely by a stream of obscenities.

Officers scrambled outside, faces buried in the crooks of their arms and uniforms covered with what had once been a painter. One policeman fell to his knees and gagged, while others stooped over, hands on knees, taking in large gulps of air.

"What the devil?" Jonathan shouted.

"A gust of wind — slammed the bedroom door — body went *boom*," one of the officers managed to say.

In the distance, an ambulance scrambled through stop signs and school crossings, siren blaring. Jonathan huffed with irony. "It's a little late for a code three."

"Hold still," one officer was saying to another.

"What?" was the reply as a maggot was flicked from his hair.

***

Mr. and Mrs. Smythe were questioned briefly. The Binghamton Gazette had a field day, and details regarding Mr. Espinoza fed the front page. Somewhere beneath the detritus, Emily still believed that Espinoza would have immortalized her.

"Says here he had no family," reported her husband as he read the Gazette the following Sunday.

"Mmm-hmm," Emily replied, sipping tea and wondering why it was he always got first pick of the paper.

"Says he didn't paint much the last ten years," he continued. "Ha! He was from Brazil—I always thought he was Spanish. Didn't you tell me that?"

Emily sighed heavily. Getting second-hand news was infuriating.

"They say his paintings were hedonistic and self-indulgent."

Emily had a sudden desire to take the remainder of the paper, roll it tight, and thwack her husband on the side of the head. She walked to the front porch and leaned against the railing to gaze at Espinoza's house. No one had set foot there since the cleaning crews finished their gruesome task, and they hadn't bothered picking up the abandoned newspapers.

"Trust-fund baby — says he inherited a small fortune," yelled her husband. "Guess he could afford to be self-indulgent."

His monotonous news reports drove her into the front yard, where she lifted her head to the large windows of Espinoza's bedroom. Still in her nightgown and bedroom slippers, she hugged herself, careful not to slip on the icy sidewalk as she walked slowly toward the front of his house.

The upstairs windows were eyes looking out and seeing in. She wished she had been more open-minded in the years Espinoza was immortalizing women. Perhaps he could have provided her with a child. She was forty-one now. She and Jonathan had tried repeatedly for twenty years.

"Ha." Jonathan was in the front doorway now, continuing the morning reports. "They say he was depressed because his body wouldn't take orders from his mind — impotent!"

The cat that she had since adopted was waiting to be let in. She had taken it home several times, yet it always returned. She fed it, and because of the damaged ear, she named it Van Gogh. She reached to pet the animal and tried the door. It was open and she slowly made her way up the complaining stairs.

The bed was gone — burned, she hoped.

Alone in a corner by the windows was an abandoned trowel, a steel bucket filled with dried plaster, and a dirty drop cloth. The walls were freshly painted, and the ceiling had received a new layer of plaster.

She surveyed the room, imagining herself on his bed, his brush waving, adding dabs of color, swerving to place the curves, transferring her essence to the canvas. In her deepest fantasy, a younger Mr. Espinoza abandoned the pallet and joined her there on the bed.

Her attention was sidetracked by a small oval of plaster that had fallen from the ceiling above where Espinoza's bed had once been. She narrowed her eyes to focus on the spot until she was clear about what it was. Emily felt the blood draining from her face.

"Don't be a fool." She steeled herself and inverted the bucket to use as a stepping stool.

After a teetering moment, she balanced and took a closer look. "An eye," she whispered.

The eye was painted well enough to appear genuine for a moment. She instinctively knew that it was the eye of Espinoza. Her discomfort was replaced by a peaceful understanding that, even in death, Mr. Espinoza still noticed her.

Emily walked back into the warmth of her kitchen.

"What a weird guy." Her husband hadn't even noticed her leaving. "It says here he had an orgy scene painted on his bedroom ceiling — workers plastered over it."

Emily burst. "He's dead, for Christ's sake!"

Jonathan cautiously lowered the paper, opened his mouth, and then shut it.

Emily clomped up the stairs, escaped into the bathroom, and cried quietly. She cried for Mr. Espinoza because no one else would. She cried for herself, for squandered opportunities and borrowed dreams.

The next morning she mixed plaster and recovered the eye of Espinoza, determined to keep it for herself.

CHAPTER 4

2016

It was a fine spring morning in Binghamton. A pair of crows busied themselves with building a stick nest on a tree-lined, gentrified street, sparing little time to laugh at the world below them.

A Hummer maneuvered down the narrow street. Bass notes blasted from the rolled down windows, causing knick-knacks to buzz and creep forward on dusty shelves. The owner pulled into his driveway on the street, opposite of what was still referred to as the Espinoza place. Prospective buyers were touring the house, and the pretty real estate specialist was talking on her cell phone from the front porch. He thought to go over for a chat because he knew her, opting instead to let T-Pain's, "*Buy U a Drank*," play out.

***

A young married couple wandered throughout the house. She was a petite Asian in her late twenties, and her husband was a tall Caucasian, ten years older. He fought the aging process with thrice-weekly workouts at a gym, and kept his hair short because it showed less grey.

"Perfect," Kiri said emphatically.

"It's a bit…Addam's Family, don't you think?" Paul murmured, staring through the upstairs windows as the Hummer-man retrieved a newspaper off the front lawn and disappeared into his house. The plate on the Hummer read, MRT2U.

"It has that lived in feeling," she

countered, swooping into the bathroom.

The smiling realtor had joined them again. "Sorry, I was expecting that call."

Paul stayed turned from the window to admire the realtor. She turned and caught him ogling, held his eyes for a moment, and smiled.

"Two sinks—no more fighting," Kiri said.

Paul cleared his throat and went into the bathroom. There was a large walk-in shower/bath combo. *Maybe things will get better here*, he thought.

"Don't you just *love* this bath?" the pretty realtor enthused. "The last owners put it in."

"Yes," Kiri said.

"I'm going to let you two wander around," the realtor grinned. It was the last room of the tour, and intuition seemed to advise her that it was a good time for them to be alone. She smiled radiantly and turned to the stairs.

"Great," Kiri smiled back at her.

They were the kind of smiles that Paul hated — a dutiful showing of teeth. When the realtor was out of hearing range, Kiri gushed, "Oh Paul, I love it! We can each have an office in the other bedrooms until...." The words caught in her throat.

"We can try out the big bath," Paul interceded, wiggling his eyebrows. "You can even lay down in there."

"One track mind." She puckered her lips and shook her head, descending the stairs ahead of him and strolling into the kitchen. Through the window, Paul saw the realtor talking on her cell phone beneath a mature maple tree.

"So, you like it?" he asked.

"It feels homey, don't you think?" She threw her arms around him and kissed him. It seemed like forever since she had kissed him like that, and it effectively lowered his defenses.

"It's possible…," he began as she rested her head against his chest.

"What?" she whispered.

"That this cooking island could be used for *making* bacon instead of slicing it." Paul backed her toward the large, granite-topped rectangle in the middle of the kitchen.

"Baby, the realtor," she giggled, and squirmed out of his grasp.

"She's yakking." His lips found her neck and he lifted her short skirt.

"Paul." She flattened her hands against his chest and pushed him back. "Seriously, what do you think?" She gestured at the updated modern appliances and did a twirl.

Paul let out a frustrated sigh. "Did you hear the music across the street?" Kiri shifted impatiently on her legs. "Okay, okay, if it makes you happy, let's do it."

Kiri crashed into his arms. "I love you!"

Absently he remembered her spewing those words when he had bought her birthday Lexis, and more recently the fourth-anniversary pearl necklace.

"Me too, deary," he rhymed her name.

Paul was an educated upper middle-class man married into an old money Japanese-American family. Before he met Kiri, he had taught junior college English for twelve years, and now he dabbled—a little of this and a little of that. A frustrated writer, his two published novels had met with tepid reviews and were quickly sentenced to the bargain book bins. Now, he helped look after her investments, which were many.

Kiri dabbled too. She helped supervise her father's business interests and property holdings, two clothing retailers, and a trendy shoe shop in Manhattan. Recently she had considered trying her hand in the import/export business because she enjoyed traveling.

Gentrification made strange bedfellows. Kiri's Lexus fit nicely in the modified carriage house. Old and new together felt right—the past shaking hands with the present. Paul hoped the same held true in the new bedroom. Two years previous, a doctor had patiently detailed to Kiri why she would have difficulty getting pregnant with Paul.

"You see, Kiri," the specialist explained. "Some men just don't produce enough sperm. The fact is sperm counts are declining worldwide. We don't exactly know why—"

Paul cut in. "What the doctor's trying to say is, I'm shooting blanks."

"Yes, well, that's one way to look at it. There are options you should consider—invitro, adoption, a donor...."

"Christ," Paul complained. "We can put

a man on the moon...."

Kiri's sexual appetite evaporated upon hearing the news. In the Japanese culture, creating a family is connected to stability and good karma. Subsequently, their lovemaking evolved into a periodic relief valve for Paul provided by a dutiful wife. His love for Kiri was strong, yet part of him was resentful. Lately, his eyes had been window-shopping, moving almost imperceptibly toward a new investment — something discreet and less complicated.

The realtor rejoined them as they mentally placed furniture in the large living room.

"We'll take it," said Kiri.

The realtor beamed. "I had a feeling you would."

CHAPTER 5

Escrow closed, and soon a semi-truck arrived with their worldly possessions—a mix of new and old to feed their interest in both. Kiri placed crisp new sheets on the antique four-poster bed as a company man placed a satellite dish in a secluded spot along the roofline. The first night Kiri was exhausted from the move, yet knew that Paul would be expecting payback. She placed a dollop of jelly on his cock and rode him to a quick conclusion. Then they slept soundly.

The earthquake struck at three-thirty in the morning, shaking the bed and rattling the windows.

"What the — ?" Paul sat up as the lamps on the night tables buzzed.

Kiri rolled out of bed and got to her feet moments before it subsided. "Oh my God, what was that?" Her hand covered her heart.

"Apparently California hasn't cornered the earthquake market," Paul quipped. Something dropped from the ceiling and landed in Paul's hair. "Jesus." He slapped at it and groped for a light.

"What is it?"

"Something fell on me."

"It better not be a cockroach — I hate cockroaches."

He found a piece of plaster that had dislodged from the ceiling above the bed.

"Earthquake damage — call FEMA," he joked.

Kiri squinted, "This is strange...."

"Easy to fix," he replied. "Even I can do

it."

"No, there's something funny." She turned on the other lamp and stood on the bed.

"Watch out for aftershocks." He nudged the bed with his knee.

"Ah!" screamed Kiri, losing her balance and falling to the bed. "That is so not funny," yet she giggled in spite of herself. Then she made it to her feet again.

"What is it?"

"It's…it's an eye."

He got on the bed beside her. "By Jove, *eye* believe you're right."

"You think it's part of a mural?"

"*Eye*'ve no idea," he answered.

"Very funny."

"We should try to get back to sleep… or…." He pulled Kiri into his arms.

"Yes, we should sleep."

***

Kiri was up at dawn. Paul watched her dress through squinting eyes. "It's Saturday...why are you up so early?"

"I want to see," she said, looking at the ceiling.

"See what?"

"If there's more."

"You're going to make a huge mess," he scolded.

"Go make some coffee and don't worry."

Grumbling, Paul did as he was asked. Through the kitchen window he saw the neighbor across the street in warm-ups begin jogging down the street. He was reminded that he still needed to join a gym in town.

"Can you bring me up a butter knife?"

"Jesus," Paul muttered.

Kiri had laid a spare sheet over the bed. Tiptoeing with the butter knife, she carefully freed a thin layer from around the eye as Paul sipped coffee. *How ironic*, he thought. She hated messes—always had to have a hand towel at the ready each time they made love.

"Look," she called out. "A nose, part of another eye, the mouth. I need something better to work with."

"Beg your pardon?" He was growing angry.

She paused to give him a pouty smile. "Please?"

"That sounded so much better." His mouth tightened.

In the kitchen, he rummaged through a toolbox and found a metal spatula. He refilled his coffee and poured her another cup as well. He would see where this martyrdom would lead. She took sugar in hers. He searched in the cupboard and spotted the Mexican yam tablets he had purchased at a nutrition shop. Having read on the Internet that it might stimulate the female libido, he had talked her into trying. They shared a space with several other concoctions, none of which kept their promises.

"Spanish fly," he chuckled mirthfully, "I wonder if that stuff really works."

When he returned, the blinds were open and Kiri was reaching high above her head to liberate plaster. The effort lifted her nightshirt to reveal a bikini panty.

"Maybe we can borrow a ladder from the neighbor." She flopped her tired arms at her side. "Then we can move the bed."

"What is it with all the *we*? Here." He handed her the coffee and watched her chip away. After twenty minutes, he went to the window and saw the black neighbor across the street standing at his upstairs balcony, still wearing his warm-ups. "Jesus, put something on...the neighbor across the street is admiring the view."

"A peeping Tom?" She hopped from the

bed and ran to the window as the neighbor retreated into his house.

"I wouldn't exactly call it peeping."

She smiled sheepishly, like a child caught stealing from the cookie jar. She led him by the hand back to the bed. His hopes escalated until she pointed. "Look, his other eye and part of a chest." She gestured to an area just below the sternum.

"Very nice. Let's call someone to come and fix it."

"Aren't you even the least bit curious?" she asked coolly.

He felt like a jerk. After all, wasn't he the creative one? "All right, I'll buy a ladder." Paul thought to use a trip to the hardware store as an excuse to pop in on the pretty realtor.

"And coffee," Kiri reminded him. "Make sure it's organic."

He pretended to write on his hand and

took the stairs by twos.

"Could you put on some classical too?" she yelled after him.

He opened a laptop on the kitchen table and signed into Spotify. Wireless Bose speakers brought Beethoven's Third Symphony, *Erotica*, to life in every room. He fired up his Jeep Cherokee and took to the road.

Cassandra was the realtor's name. She had short bleach-blonde hair, and preferred *not* to be called Cassy. She didn't have showings that day, and seemed pleased to see Paul walk into the office that she shared with three other realtors. When he inquired about the mural, she hedged. "Have you had breakfast yet?"

Central Park Cafe was three hours upstate from Manhattan, but the coffee was top notch. Paul detailed the effects of the earthquake and the subsequent revelation.

"I didn't even wake up. My husband says I sleep like the dead." Cassandra's meticulously painted eyes were wide with feigned wonder.

"Do you know anything about the history of our house? Kiri told me to ask," he fibbed.

"You guys look so adorable together." She flashed her generic smile. "She's so tiny next to you."

"Yes," he replied, "we're the odd couple."

"Well, about the house," she began. "The rumor mill is full of juicy tidbits." She raised her eyebrows and wiggled in her chair.

"How juicy?" He propped his chin up with a fist.

"Can I get you anything to go with your coffee?" a waiter queried. "Some quiche perhaps? We also have—"

"Nothing for me, thanks," Paul

interrupted.

"I'm fine," Cassandra answered, raising a defensive hand. She noticed Paul glancing at her T-shirt and the *Hollister* logo stretched across her ample breasts. "Okay, first the facts. The Simmons family lived there for five years before you bought it, but long before that, in the late forties and early fifties, a painter owned the house."

"*Our* painter?"

She nodded. "His name was Espinoza. I think he was Spanish or something."

"And?" Paul surrounded her with his eyes as she leaned back in her chair to cross her legs. Designer jeans looked as if they had been airbrushed over her long thin legs. *This one is a man-eater*, he thought.

"I heard that he was a party animal—had weird people in and out of the house at all hours. His paintings were considered pornography in those days. I've never seen one." She curtained her eyes.

"Where can I find his work?"

"Well, there is one lady in town that's supposed to have a sizable collection."

"Yeah? Where can I find her?"

"Let me finish." She held up a finger. "This is just hearsay, mind you." She smiled mischievously. Paul leaned forward with his hands folded in his lap. "Well, I was told that Espinoza became impotent, and judging from his lifestyle that was a death sentence."

"How did he die?" Paul inquired.

"He stopped wanting to live and starved himself."

"Viagra would've saved his life," Paul observed wryly.

"You're probably right. So...." She touched his leg. "When are you going to show me this painting of yours?"

"I'll give you an exclusive tour when

Kiri's demolition work is finished."

"Promise me," her voice crinkled sensuously. "I'll bring a bottle of wine."

"What about the lady you were telling me about?"

Cassandra took a sip of coffee and held his eyes. "I was saving that for last—she lives right next door to you."

"Jesus, what am I getting into?" He shook his head.

"Hey." She touched his shoulder and let her fingers flow down to his bicep. "My husband and I bought a brand new house last year with no history whatsoever. Yours came ready-made. It will always be the *Espinoza* house. The only way to get my house remembered is to murder my husband in the shower."

"Have you thought about it?"

"A few times," she smiled.

CHAPTER 6

Kiri was lying on her stomach across the bed when Paul returned. Her long black hair was dotted with white shards of plaster.

"How's it going? Should I call the Smithsonian?" he said, feeling guilty about forgetting the organic coffee. He handed her the gouging trowel that the hardware man claimed would do the job.

"My arms got tired." She shrugged her shoulders in circles and massaged the back of her neck.

"Ah," he sympathized, straddling her back to rub her shoulders. "Poor, weary Kiri."

He tipped his head and saw a man's face staring down at him, twisted into a mask of conflicted emotions. The mouth was curved into an exaggerated expression of either pain or pleasure. The eyes competed in a tug-of-war between darkness and light. Even with these strange variations, the face was roughly handsome. Paul's hands stopped moving and Kiri reached back and prodded him to continue.

"What do you think it is?" he asked.

"I don't know."

"I wonder how much more there is."

"If it's a mural," she said, "then there could be a lot more."

"Our own little Sistine Chapel." He kneaded her shoulders. His thoughts wandered to Cassandra as Kiri moaned appreciatively. How would her voice sound during an orgasm? Orgasms were thumbprints — every woman had her own distinct sound.

"I have to go the city tomorrow."

"Are you flying?" Paul asked.

"I think I'll drive my birthday present this time. The forecast looks okay."

"Are you staying with your sister?"

"Yes."

"Want to fool around?"

"Maybe when I get back."

"Rain-check?"

"Rain-check."

The following morning, Kiri readied herself for the trip. Paul made what was left of the coffee they had and she couldn't tell the difference. She was all business.

"What kind of business do you have?" he asked as she bit into a bagel with cream cheese.

"I have to do a big shakeup at one of the clothing stores."

"Do you want me to go?"

"I already told my sister I was spending the night with her." She sipped fresh-squeezed carrot juice.

"I'll work a bit on your mural," he volunteered, which made her smile.

"Don't scrape, or you'll damage the paint—just pry and peel," she advised. "It comes off pretty easily."

"I'll call Bob Villa if I run into a problem."

"Who's that?"

"A famous homewrecker," he answered.

She kissed him and clicked out in high heels. Her short skirt was wrapped like a cocoon around her upper thighs, and the burgundy blouse was pure silk. Kiri made anything she wore look good, Paul reflected. Across the street, the neighbor was sitting on his balcony reading a paper. Paul watched him lower it to stare as she got into the car.

Paul showered and strolled over to the next-door neighbor's. If there were any truth in the story Cassandra had told, he would have another excuse to visit her office.

A smiling woman in her early eighties greeted his knock.

"Hi, I'm your new neighbor, Paul O'Neil."

She accepted his hand and he could feel it trembling. "It's a pleasure to meet you, Mr. O'Neil. I'm Emma...Emma Gorman. Please call me Em." Her eyes sparkled. "Thank you so much for stopping by. The Simmons lived in that house for five years, and I never even met them."

"Everybody lives in their own world, I guess," Paul said.

"And with all this technology, cell phones and the like, it's only getting worse."

"I agree with you."

"Would you like to come in? I have some fresh baked peanut butter cookies."

"Thank you, peanut butter cookies are

one of my favorites." He followed her into the kitchen. The layout of her house looked about the same as his, but with a dining area.

"Would you like some milk to go with them?"

"No thanks, Mrs. Gorman." He took a bite. "Mmm, these are wonderful."

"My mother's recipe."

"I understand that you own a collection of famous paintings."

"The Espinozas," she finished. "And I believe the word is *in*famous. Would you like to see them?"

"Actually, I would." Paul smiled at his good fortune.

"I can't remember the last time anyone wanted to see them." She led him to the stairs.

"I appreciate you sharing them with me," he said.

"Better save it until you see them." She

turned to pat his arm. "They're not exactly everyone's cup of tea." The stairs creaked and complained as they slowly made their way up. "I'm an only child, born nine months after Mr. Espinoza died. Isn't that something?"

"It is," he agreed politely as they reached the top of the stairs.

"My parents told me that they had almost given up trying."

"So, Mr. Espinoza's death brought them some luck," Paul said.

"I s'pose." She pointed to a small bedroom. "I sleep here, and the paintings are in the master suite." She stopped before the door and put a palsied hand on his shoulder. "Let me explain something so you don't get the wrong impression. These paintings were my mother's, God rest her soul."

Paul nodded and opened the door,

and she turned on the light for him. Three walls were nearly covered with paintings of various sizes. His senses were immediately swamped by an abundance of flesh.

"Wow." He immediately focused on the painting of a redhead in an armchair. Her feet were planted on the armrests and she was diddling herself, with her head thrown back and mouth flung open. Espinoza's looping, crisscrossing signature was large and black at the lower right corner, with the year 1946 crammed next to it. Another work portrayed a man seated on a pillow, legs crossed in a lotus position, his penis draped heavily over the left thigh. Next was the painting of an orgy, faces twisted in rapture, a veritable guidebook to sexual positioning. "Whew."

"Yes," Mrs. Gorman smiled. "They have that effect."

Paul crabbed along the walls, his eyes filling with one decadent maelstrom of sexuality after another. "I take it these weren't too popular in their time," he said almost to himself.

"Nor any thereafter," she remarked. "I tried selling them a few years back to create a college trust for my grandchildren—had a young appraiser over. He took one look and advised me to put them on one of those Internet whatchamacallit's...."

"EBay," Paul finished.

"Well, you can bet I didn't offer *him* any peanut butter cookies." She chuckled at the memory. "He went on to lecture me that Espinoza had questionable brush skills."

"How did your mother...?"

"She was an odd one, God rest her soul. She had different ideas about what constituted art. She took her reasons for liking the Espinozas to her grave."

Paul didn't press further, not wanting to come off sounding like an investigative reporter. He peered closer to a painting of two women making love among autumn leaves, and an obscure face spying through a stand of bushes.

"My father was very conservative, and he hated Espinoza with a passion. My mother called Espinoza's the happy house — lots of parties, music, and laughter at all hours. This is Espinoza's only self-portrait." She pointed to the opposite wall, arranged so that the viewer would have little choice but to look into Espinoza's strange eyes...the same eyes that kept watch over Paul's bed.

"Did she purchase all of these after Espinoza's death?"

Emma laughed. "No, no, no...she found them in the dumpster they used when they were renovating the house. I guess he kept the paintings in the attic, and when the workers found them — well, here they are."

"Yet you said that your father hated

Espinoza."

She laughed again. "Mother hid them in *our* attic. She had been after Father to clean that thing out for years and he never did, so she knew the paintings would be safe there."

"I'll be darned." Paul loved the way Emma told stories, and stored them away to use in his writing later. "Em, I can't tell you what a pleasure it's been. I have some business to do, but I'd like to bring my wife over to see these if it's okay."

"Any time. I'm always here, and Mr. Espinoza certainly isn't going anywhere."

CHAPTER 7

"'Curiouser and curiouser,'" Paul quoted *Alice in Wonderland* as he walked home. Then he saw the mail truck stuffing the community-block mailboxes…a beehive containing twenty-five cells. He and Kiri shared cell fifteen. Paul greeted the mail carrier and waited patiently. The tall black man from across the street joined him.

"How's you doin'?" The man smiled. "You just moved in, right?"

"Yeah." Paul reached to take his hand. "I'm Paul O'Neil."

"Bobby Thornton." His hand engulfed Paul's.

Paul shook a finger with recognition, "Wait a minute." He narrowed his eyes. "Are you *the* Bobby Thornton?" Now he noticed the World Series ring on his left hand.

"The one and only," Bobby nodded, proud to be remembered ten years after his retirement from major league baseball.

"Wow, I watched you play with the Yanks. You were really something."

"Thanks Paul. Listen, I gotta scoot, but we'll have to get together real soon."

"Any Bobby Juniors coming up the ranks?"

"I got a son, but he's not into ball." Thornton shifted nervously on his feet.

"Well, it was great to meet you," Paul said. "We'll have you over for some wine," he added lamely.

"That's a good game plan," Bobby called back, already halfway across the street. Then he stopped. "I played ball with *another* Paul O'Neil…remember him?" he yelled.

"Who could forget?" Paul answered.

Wow, thought Paul, *wait until Kiri hears that it was Bobby Thornton watching her in her underwear*. As he reached the door, will.i.am, started blasting, "I Got it From My Mama" behind the Hummer's privacy glass as it glided out of the driveway and into the street.

***

Paul was prying plaster from the ceiling when Kiri returned late the next evening. He heard her put away groceries, and then the tattletale stairs announced every step of her approach. He descended the ladder to give her a kiss.

"How's the project coming?"

"Hey there." He liked the way she looked from up there. "You were right, this stuff flakes off pretty easily."

"Want me to spell you?"

"You just got home. Don't you want to rest?"

"Let me change first," and she disappeared into the walk-in closet.

"Did you fire the clothing store manager?"

"We had a heart-to-heart and I gave her another shot."

"Good for you."

"Where did you put the coffee? I was going to make some fresh, but I didn't find it."

She emerged from the closet wearing one of his long-sleeved white dress shirts. Women look fabulous in a man's dress shirt, he observed. "I met our neighbor across the street."

"Yeah?"

"You'll never guess who he is."

"A hip-hop star?"

"No, Bobby Thornton."

Kiri scrunched up her forehead, but the name didn't ring a bell.

"He played for the Yanks."

"Did he see me the other day?"

"He posted you on YouTube," Paul quipped.

"Ha, ha, ha," she droned, climbing up the ladder.

"I invited him for wine."

"When?"

"We didn't set a time yet."

"Oh." She was quickly immersed in the mural.

"I ran into the old lady next door, Mrs. Gorman."

"Uh-huh." Her voice had the empty quality of pretending to listen.

"I'm going to fuck the real estate lady," he teased.

"What, baby?"

"Nothing," he amended. "Just making a mental note to myself."

She took a sharp breath. "Oh my goodness."

Her tone drew his attention to the mural, where a large penis was penetrating the yawning lips of a hirsute pussy.

"Very nice," Paul mocked. "I'll call Hustler." He stalked to the door. "I'm going out for the coffee."

CHAPTER 8

"What's eating him?" she asked the face of Espinoza. "Penis envy," she smiled smugly. She slipped the spatula under another section and a large piece fell to the sheet. "Incredible," she breathed, reaching out to touch the distended member. She felt a raised relief of veins. A dark haired woman straddled the magnificent staff with her back to him. Kiri felt the ridges of the woman's sphincter. The whole scene, intuition told her, was a mirror image of the reality that took place on the bed many years ago.

Kiri worked until the entire scene was

freed and she could clearly make out a large pillow resting beneath the man's lower back. She gawked at the enormous size of the penis and wondered what it would feel like. Judging from the woman's expression it would feel very good. Kiri's fingers slid beneath the waistband of her panty and she felt dampness there. "Where the hell did Paul say he was going?" she queried the woman in the mural.

***

The realtor's office was on the way to get coffee. He parked and keyed the alarm on the Cherokee — *his* car, Kiri took pleasure in reminding him. Cassandra's Audi was parked at the office, and as luck had it she was alone, chatting on the phone. She beamed him her best laser smile and lifted a *be right with you* finger. Then she used a charming falsetto to finish the conversation.

"Indy Jones, how's the archeological dig

coming?" she joked.

"Wish I had his money," he grinned. "I came by to tell you about my visit to Mrs. Gorman."

"The porno queen?"

"You're not very far off. Those paintings were pretty—"

"Hot?" she finished.

"Scorching," he added.

"When are you going to show me the bedroom mural?" She glanced at his crotch.

"Soon, I promise."

Cassandra leaned back in her chair. "Your wife is adorable."

Paul knew that Cassandra was testing him. "Yes she is."

She bit her lower lip, "Would you like a Diet Pepsi?"

She led him to the conference room, where a refrigerator stood. Brown leather chairs were dutifully shoved in around the large meeting table. They popped their cans and sipped as Paul pored over the calendar in his head. She stood close, invading his space...he liked having his space invaded. Her perfume made his head float like spider webs on a breeze.

"Next Tuesday, why don't you stop by?" he suggested, remembering that Kiri had another trip planned to the city.

"Let me check." Her heels clicked on the tile as she returned to her desk.

"Kiri will be out of town on business, but if it works out for you...."

Cassandra flipped the pages of her date book without really looking at them. "Tuesday's perfect," she finished. "What time?"

He suppressed a belch, redirecting it painfully through his nose. He hated diet drinks. "Ten?"

"Great." She lowered her eyelids. "I'm a

morning person."

He wondered if she noticed his heart pounding in his Adam's apple, or screaming behind his zipper.

Stupid fuck, Paul reprimanded himself as he drove home. *You're getting into deep shit – think divorce, loss of income, returning to the classroom.* His hands were trembling as he drove past the shop that carried organic coffee.

CHAPTER 9

Kiri had gathered up the protective sheet and lay on the bed admiring the mural. Moistening a finger, she reached down to find the almond-sliver of her clitoris and shivered with pleasure. The front door opened.

"Paul, get up here," she yelled feverishly.

"Shit, what now?" he agonized softly. The coffee! He slapped the front of his head with the palm of his hand.

"Paul!" she beckoned.

"Coming!"

***

She was writhing on the bed when

he arrived. He quickly fumbled with his clothing.

"Hurry baby, get inside me."

Paul cupped his hands under her knees to lift her legs and pushed down and in.

"Ayyy!" Her voice was deep, almost masculine. Staring at the mural, she came almost immediately, bucking uncontrollably and digging her heels into his kidneys. "Hyyy," she screamed as another orgasm gripped her.

Paul was beside himself with pleasure, and after a few minutes he sent a stream of penniless soldiers deep inside his thrashing wife. A few minutes later, he slipped out and they lay facing each other.

Finally, she broke the reverie. "What a mess." She stemmed the flow of semen with her hand. "And these sheets are new."

Paul hopped from bed and brought back a warm washcloth. She let him clean her—

he kissed her there and her fingers stroked his head encouragingly. She tasted salty and smelled like chlorine. He flicked his tongue and she arched her back to let him know that he was cruising the right address.

After Kiri was satiated, she curled into him. They napped until the pockmarked half-moon cast the dancing shadows of a tree into the room. He listened to her breathing, rhythmical and contented. There was still dampness on the top-sheet.

Now he felt complete, loved her, and never should have doubted that she would find her way back to him. Tomorrow he would cancel his Tuesday appointment with the realtor.

Early the next morning Kiri greeted him with a kiss and the morning paper. "I wanted to make coffee, but—"

He kissed her again. "You know how much I love you?"

"I think I have a pretty good idea," she grinned. "That reminds me, I'm meeting with my father on Tuesday and staying at Yoshi's for a night or two—girl stuff, you know."

"Yeah, I remember you saying something about that a while back."

"You can work on the mural while I'm gone."

Paul wasn't in the mood to talk about the mural.

"I haven't felt this good in...." He paused.

"Since...?" she added.

He smiled. "Do you still want a baby?"

She nodded, holding back tears.

"Okay. One way or another, I swear we'll make it happen."

She hugged him tightly.

"I forgot the coffee," he admitted.

"Let's go buy some together."

They dressed and he drove her Lexus to the grocery store. When they returned, Paul put away groceries while Kiri brewed coffee. There was a knock at the door.

"I'll get it, darling," she volunteered. "Finish putting the tall stuff away."

CHAPTER 10

"Hey there, you must be Paul's wife, I'm Bobby — Bobby Thornton."

"Kiri." His hand swallowed hers. "Very nice to meet you. My husband says you are a football player."

"Baseball — but you were in the ballpark," he smiled, and lifted a wine gift bag. "A little sumpin' to welcome you to the neighborhood."

Paul joined them and shook the huge hand. "Hey, Bobby, how's it going? What a great surprise…what's this?" He gestured to the bag.

"Just a little sumpin'."

"Thanks," he smiled. "Please come in."

"Yeah, I learned a little about wine when we played in Canada," he explained.

Paul glanced at his watch. "It's almost eleven…let's open it."

Bobby checked his Rolex. "Maybe just a sip."

"I'll get glasses," Kiri offered. "Make yourselves comfortable."

"I haven't been in here since Letty — uh, the Simmons family — moved out."

Paul led him to the leather sofas in the living room. "We haven't had time to do much to the place yet," he apologized.

"What you do, Paul?" Bobby queried.

"Oh, a little of this, little of that. I dabble in real estate and do a little writing on the side. How long have you lived here?" he redirected the conversation.

"Going on ten years — moved here after my divorce. You know how that goes," he nodded.

Paul didn't know, yet nodded in agreement. Kiri arrived with glasses and a corkscrew. Paul popped the cork and they toasted.

"Here's to stayin' positive and testing negative," Bobby said.

"So — you play baseball," Kiri said.

"Retired," he corrected. "Ten years and three teams."

"Bobby was one of the best outfielders in the game," Paul nodded.

"Well, I don't know about that," he smiled.

"Who was toughest to hit?" Paul inquired.

"Hard to say — Randy Johnson, Roger Clemens, those guys were almost untouchable." He narrowed his eyes. "Johnson…whew, left-handed side-arm delivery, comin' outta nowhere, a hundred miles an hour."

Kiri didn't understand, but Bobby was handsome and his voice sounded deep and rich. Bobby relaxed, leaned forward to talk baseball, and she refilled his glass. Her sister, Yoshi, had confided about an affair she'd had with a black businessman. She would have to ask for details on Tuesday.

Bobby quickly finished his glass. "Gotta scoot folks, but I'll cook up some ribs at my place real soon."

"Are you sure you have to go? I have an eighteen-year-old Scotch," Paul tempted.

"I got a gig, but I'll take a rain check." He shook Paul's hand and took both of Kiri's to say farewell, adding a kiss to the cheek.

They watched him jog across the street to fire up the Hummer. Rapper 50 Cent was making his point abundantly clear with a liberal dusting of profuse language and threats of great bodily harm.

***

That night as they listened to Schubert's String Quartet, Paul suggested plastering over the mural.

"Why?" she demanded.

"Jeez…I mean, won't you get tired of waking up to that every morning?" He flung his hands up toward the ceiling.

"You sound so Republican," she snipped.

Paul flushed with anger. "All right, forget it."

His subsequent sexual advances were met with the usual rebuff. "Goodnight, deary," he said, seeking closure.

"Night." And she turned on her side away from him.

CHAPTER 11

Molasses Monday slowly closed shop. Kiri had packed an overnighter...she was taking an early morning *puddle-jumper* to the City. Paul lay in bed obsessing as Kiri brushed her teeth. He hadn't canceled with Cassandra. Every time he thought to, her voice reached out subliminally. "I'm a morning person." It's just a game, he convinced himself, and I'll play a hand or two, lay down the cards, and cut my losses.

Tuesday morning Kiri was business as usual. She consulted her cell phone, kissed him mechanically, and was out the door and into a waiting taxi.

"Work on the mural, it's nearly finished," she yelled out the window.

"Oui oui, mademoiselle." He blew her a kiss.

He glanced out the living room window when he returned inside. Bobby was taking out the trash and the taxi paused for Kiri to chat briefly. He smiled, nodded, and waved her off. Paul began flip-flopping about his morning date with Cassandra, yet the results of the debate were lopsided in favor of his erection.

***

Cassandra looked at the family portrait on her desk—two youngsters, Nash and Tyler, standing between her and Bill. She was smiling in the photo. She wondered how marriages became leftover Christmas wrapping paper. Paul O'Neil was handsome and witty. He was the reason she was wearing her red thong. Paul O'Neil, sexy and passionate, and definitely not Bill. Cassandra primped in the office mirror, touched up her short-cropped blonde hair, warmed up her silver Audi, and drove away from Christmas wrap.

***

Paul tried showering away his nervousness, but it returned as soon as he toweled off. He carefully cut his toenails, rounded them off, and dug out the edges with a file. He clipped his fingernails, trimmed his pubic hair, and shaved the hair from the bottom of his shaft.

Jesus, he thought, *what is it about marriage that makes a man stop caring about how he looks?* He walked into the closet and chose a pair of loose fitting black linen pants, matching them with a black silk shirt.

A chilled bottle of Sauvignon Blanc stood at attention on the living room coffee table. White wine was always a safe bet with most women. If she preferred something else, he had that too. Spotify filled the rooms with smooth jazz.

He was touching cologne to his neck when he heard her car pull into the driveway. Cassandra stood at the door with a fabric wine bag and a genuinely dazzling smile.

"We haven't done much decorating yet," he explained, seeing her practiced eyes scanning the rooms.

"It takes time to put a house like this together," she nodded. "Is Bobby Thornton still across the street?"

"Yes, he was just over. Interesting man; you know him?"

"Yes indeed," she said with vague smile. "Yes, he is very interesting."

"What would you like to drink?"

She lifted the bag for him. "How about we start with this?"

Paul showed her into the living room

and lifted out a bottle of premium tequila. "Nice," he said. "I'll get the shot glasses."

"Don't bother." She opened her purse and took out two.

"You surprise me."

"Why is that?"

Instead of replying, he poured two shots, handed her glass, and raise his. "Salud."

"Salud," she repeated.

"Let's bring our drinks upstairs and I'll show you the mural."

"Lead on." She arched her eyebrows. "I've been looking forward to this all week." She grabbed the bottle.

"Me too," he said as they walked up the creaking stairs. He stopped at the threshold of the bedroom for a toast.

"Here's to the arts," he said.

"To the passions they inspire," she amended.

They touched glasses. "After you." He

opened the door for her.

"Oh my god," she said, her head lifting higher the closer she got to the mural. "This is really...." Paul stood close, smelling her perfume. He could almost taste the back of her neck. "I'm speechless—it's like a mirror image. Just a second...." She set her wine on the night stand. "Do you mind?" She removed her heels and lay on the bed, crossing her legs at the ankles.

"Be my guest," Paul said, his brain turning into mush.

"Oh yes, definitely. This is how it's meant to be seen."

His erection pressed unashamedly against his slacks. She uncrossed her ankles and lifted a knee as she gazed at the mural. Paul could make out the beginnings of her red underwear. "Mind if I join you?"

"Of course not."

He lay next to her and they stared

quietly at the cosmos of flesh. She reached for his hand. "Thank you for sharing this." She turned on her side toward him. "It's amazing."

"So are you."

"You think so?" Her hand touched his face. The first kiss was tender and their tongues danced slowly. Paul slipped a hand beneath her blouse to find the catch. She unbuttoned his shirt and soon there was a jumble of clothing strewn all about. The kisses gained length and appetite. As her panties came down, he was faced with a carefully sculpted, blonde sanctuary and visited there with his tongue.

"Oh yeah, right there—yeah, ahhh," she purred as he flicked her fleshy teardrop. Her thighs clamped and quivered around his head and her breath issued in short, jerky spurts.

The aftertaste of the tequila mingled with

her juices to create a sensual symphony. "Mmm, you taste good," he mumbled.

Gently, she pushed his head away and got to her knees. "Lay back," she said. Cassandra, never confused with Cassy or any variation thereof, impaled herself on his cock.

Paul panicked. The urge to cum was incontestable. He trapped her hips with his hands, yet she found a way to keep moving. He pictured the dishes in the sink, thought about his upcoming meeting with a financial advisor, but nothing helped. He grunted and swamped her with premature ejaculate.

"Did you—?" Cassandra looked down, looking bewildered. Paul tried to stay inside, stroked himself, sucked her nipples, and willed another erection, yet his soldier was insubordinate. She sighed, lifted off him, and sat on the side of the bed.

"Sorry, you just felt so damn—"

"It's okay." She drained her shot-glass.

"Just give it a few minutes." He poured another.

"Actually, I have an appointment—rain-check?"

"Sure," he said lamely.

She gave him her best counterfeit smile and excused herself to the bathroom. Paul felt himself stirring again. While gazing at the neat little circle of moisture on the bedspread, his penis hardened. When she returned he stood to face her with a lascivious grin fixed on his face.

"Ready for a do-over?"

She smiled as if she were showing a house—the same courtesy smile you find at checkout stands. "Sorry, I really have to run."

"Sure, rain check," he deadpanned.

She kissed him politely. "I'll let myself out." Pointing to his shot glass, she said,

"You should finish that—it's very tasty."

"I'll give you a ring," he said desperately.

The front door closed, and from the bedroom window he watched her slide into the Audi and peel out as she left the curb.

"Idiot," he screamed. "Ten-seconds!" He glared down at his penis and it mocked him by filling with blood again. A ten second ride may win a rodeo, but it certainly didn't win hearts.

CHAPTER 12

Kiri leaped into his arms like a child when she returned the following evening, thus magnifying Paul's guilt a thousand-fold. Guilt cost an expensive flower arrangement for Kiri. He had an anonymous one sent to Cassandra too, just to smooth things over. Tickets to the symphony lay on the dining room table for Kiri to discover. Guilt also included a dry cleaning bill for the bedspread. He'd finished the tequila off after Cassandra left, and he was also paying for that.

Paul welcomed Kiri into his arms, "Nice to see you too." Without a word she handed him her suitcase and led him up the stairs. She didn't notice the flowers, and he wished now that he had placed them in the bedroom.

"I have a surprise," she announced with a coy smile. "Put the suitcase on the bed."

Paul flopped her suitcase on the bed and Kiri hurriedly unzipped it. She lifted a layer of clothing, revealing a faux-leather briefcase. "When they ran it through X-ray, a lady security guard opened it, smiled, and then closed it again. Then she smiled and said, 'Have a good flight.' I was *so* embarrassed."

"You have my undivided attention." Paul lifted the case and shook it.

"Careful!" She gripped the case and put it on the bed.

His eyes narrowed. "Don't I get to guess?"

"Just open it," she said.

Paul flipped down the latches and lifted the lid. The inside was lined in blue velvet, and a large instruction booklet was laid over the contents.

Paul read the bold letters, Pandora's Box, then the smaller type, Everything you need is *here* to get you *there*. Listed below, framed by a pair of cheap-looking blondes, it read, This Kit Includes: 1 Black 8"x 2" black Realistic dildo/w/harness, 1 bumblebee vibrator, 2 black velvet "softy" masks, 2 pairs of Velcro soft-cuffs, 1 jar of edible mango body jelly, 1 tube of EZ-in anal/vaginal lubricant, one 6" butt plug, and our illustrated suggestion guide.

Paul was flabbergasted. He shook his head, "What in God's—?"

"There was an adult store in Manhattan, close to Yoshi's apartment. We went together and I was so uncomfortable at first, but they were very nice." Kiri picked up the pamphlet and sat on the bed next to him. "I thought it would be fun to try something new."

Paul saw everything organized neatly, each item surrounded by its own protective foam. He tentatively lifted out the enormous dildo. It looked genuine, right down to the road map of veins. It even had a large pair of balls that squished around when you squeezed them.

He appraised his petite wife. "How's *this* going to work?"

She took up the lubricant and thumbed to the illustration demonstrating how the dildo fit into the harness.

"Let's find out." She slipped out of her clothes and modeled the apparatus. "See?"

Paul's penis was throbbing with sensory overload. "You'll need stitches," he argued as he removed his clothes.

She leaned her lips against his ear. "Put

it on and let's play."

Paul's head still throbbed, yet his penis had borrowed blood from the rest of his body. Kiri helped with the harness, and the dildo felt awkward and heavy. She set the kit on the nightstand within easy reach and pinned him on his back with her thighs. She blindfolded him and tethered his hands and feet to opposite bedposts.

"Kinky," he observed.

Paul's cock jutted below the balls of the dildo. Kiri took it in her hand, twisted and teased him with her tongue. Then he heard the wet sound of lubricant being smeared over the massive dark cylinder—a noise that reminded him of melted cheese being stirred into macaroni.

Kiri tugged gently at his nipples with her front teeth, and when he complained, she nipped harder. Then she mounted the thick black penis, and Paul felt her thighs tighten around his hips as she sat down, down, down.

"Hyyy, ohhh...my god." Her pleasure was discomforted at first, yet quickly changed. Her small hands gripped the hair on his chest as she lifted and then lowered herself again. "Oyyy," she cried.

Paul's erection dissolved beneath the usurping phallus, and he heard the crinkling sound of lubricant being displaced from her pussy. She lowered her hips until the entire dildo was buried within her. Kiri's voice sounded foreign to him. He wanted the blindfold off, to gaze upon this strange apparition, this latest version of his wife. As if on cue she removed it and placed it over her own eyes.

Good god, he marveled, *she took every inch of that thing.* Kiri's voice grew husky and frenzied as she sent the cock in and out of her. Paul's cock slinked away to hide safety between his thighs.

"Ohhh, god, I'm gonna cum!" she announced, shuddering and screeching like a hawk circling in the sky. She twisted her nipples and bucked with each successive orgasm.

Paul was pelted with sweat as her head swung side-to-side, hair swishing and brushing his face. She was in an alternate universe, and Paul desperately wished he could join her there. With a final quiver, Kiri collapsed over him.

***

Kiri's transformation should have made him giddy with delight. Instead, he realized that he was a conventional guy who just wanted conventional sex. On the other hand, Kiri had discovered her need to experiment and go beyond the realm of the ordinary. She purchased sex guides and studied how to get the best bang for her buck. She rented pornos that showcased men with impossibly large cocks, making Paul regret the day he was born.

Paul's penis became unreliable, and Kiri's best efforts often met with disappointment. Sometimes after a promising start, his cock would go MIA. She began leaving information pamphlets lying around where he would find them, extolling the virtue and safety record of Viagra. He gritted his teeth and read them. He played it off as a case of jitters, and indeed he *was* nervous. He worried about bumping into Cassandra when Kiri was with him. There was no telling what might happen. He knew that women sometimes saved up, waiting for a perfect opportunity to wreak havoc.

Paul stressed about the mural as its universe expanded like a filthy big-bang theorem. The ceiling was littered with naked bodies, intertwined, engaged in every decadent act known to man and beast. Paul yearned for a return to the time when their fantasies were safe, a time when he didn't feel so goddamned inadequate.

Weeks later, before flying to New York City to combine business with a visit to his mother, he broached the subject of children again. Kiri looked right past him. They had been down this rocky road too many times. He ticked off a list of options before her face brightened with the last one.

"A sperm donor—I might go for something like that," she enthused.

Paul thought of the idea—another man's cum in his wife, someone else's baby, not his. "Okay." His voice was monotone, defeated. If things were ever going to get back to normal, he would have to swallow his pride. "Let's find out more about it."

Kiri hugged him. "I wish you wouldn't go."

"I asked you to come," he reminded.

"I know, but I thought you needed some space," she purred.

"I'll be back in a couple of days." He kissed her and felt a stirring. Cocks have a mind of their own.

***

After he left, Kiri saw Mrs. Gorman sweeping her front porch. She slipped into a comfortable pair of jeans and a T-shirt that said, *Bad Girl*. Over a month had passed since the move, and she hadn't chatted with her closest neighbor.

Mrs. Gorman grinned and straightened up slowly to welcome her. Her smile eliminated years from her face. "Kiri, what an adorable name," she said, showing her into the living area. "Would you like a dish of ice-cream? I've got mocha almond fudge."

"No thanks, Mrs. Gorman. I just stopped by to say hello."

"I'll bet you came by to see the paintings," she began. "Your husband said that he was going to bring you."

"Paintings?" she puzzled.

"Yes, dear, didn't he tell you about the Espinozas?"

"No, he never mentioned them." There was a hard edge in her voice.

"Oh well, there's a man for you," Emma laughed.

"Would you let me see them, Mrs. Gorman?"

"Only if you call me Em. My mother's name was Emily." She motioned for Kiri to come into the house. "My name is Emily, but my father shortened it to avoid confusion."

Kiri nodded. "How many paintings do you have?"

"Well, you'll see for yourself," she said as they arrived at the bedroom door. "I'll open the blinds just a bit—natural light is better to see by."

A soft morning radiance flooded the room and Kiri drew in a sharp breath. "Oh my —"

"Are you sure you won't have some ice-cream? It's too much to eat by myself," Mrs. Gorman tempted.

"Maybe just a tiny scoop." Kiri wanted to be alone, to allow the Espinozas to seep into her bloodstream.

"Comin' right up." The old woman carefully negotiated the stairs, accompanied by assorted creaks and groans.

Kiri approached the painting of a dark-skinned man standing by a Latin woman. The woman sat on a rug with his attenuated ebony staff grasped in her hand. The other hand lifted her skirt to reveal a dark thatch. The man stood proudly, as if he were looking directly into the eyes of the painter. Kiri's nipples pushed against her T-shirt, reminding her that she had neglected to wear a bra. She felt sudden warmth between her legs. Emma's voice made her jump.

"Papa wasn't aware of these. My mother rescued them from a dumpster after Espinoza died," Emma laughed, "and she hid them in the attic."

"Your father never found them?" Kiri asked.

"Nope, after he died of a stroke she hung them."

She half listened as Mrs. Gorman regaled her past, filling in the blanks that accompany old age with imaginings. The paintings transported Kiri to a time when hedonism reigned supreme and orgasms were traded like currency.

CHAPTER 13

After a self-indulgent hour, she thanked Mrs. Gorman and promised to visit again soon. Yet, Mrs. Gorman knew that it was an empty promise like the one's she got from friends and family. Cute little Kiri wouldn't be back until guilt forced her out of a sense of moral duty. You get to a certain age, she thought sadly, when you become like disappearing ink, with only the pressure marks of the pen to prove you ever existed. She rocked on the porch as Kiri strolled toward the mailboxes.

***

Bobby Thornton was dressed in warm-ups when he spotted Kiri through his bedroom window. He ran down the stairs and jogged across the street to catch up with her.

"We haven't seen you around much," Kiri smiled.

"Been busy, you know — stove-top dinners, card shows, and what-not. Hardly got time for hoops with my dawgs."

She didn't understand but smiled. "The wine you brought was excellent."

"I got some better vine at the house. Why don't you come over and we'll pop a few?"

"Paul is out of town for a few days."

"That's okay, I won't bite."

***

Mrs. Gorman thought the difference in their sizes was amusing as they walked to his house. She got up stiffly for another bowl of ice cream. Despite the chill, she didn't enjoy eating it anywhere else but the front porch.

***

Just inside the house, Kiri was confronted with baseball memorabilia, photos, plaques, and a framed uniform. In display cases there were baseballs, autographed bats, a Golden Glove award, dozens of trophies, and medals. The entryway was designed to impress upon visitors that Bobby Thornton had *been* somebody.

"Make yourself cozy, take a look around while I score some wine."

She didn't understand baseball very well. She had been a student at a private high school, taking evening ballet classes, when Bobby was smacking baseballs and making diving catches. She was finishing her undergraduate studies in economics when a knee injury terminated his career at thirty-three.

On a secluded wall, she noticed a large

family portrait of Bobby, smiling, with three young children.

"The kids are mostly grown up now, but I try to keep in touch."

Kiri nodded as he handed her a glass. She sipped and felt much better. "Mmm, this tastes wonderful."

He showed her a wall photo of him with President Clinton, and then he guided her into the living room. A black leather sofa was littered with newspapers, sports magazines, an empty Cheetos bag, and a leopard-print brassiere. He set them gingerly on the coffee table next to an empty 40 ounce beer bottle.

"Maid's day off," he explained.

"Is this French?" she sipped.

"Bordeaux," he answered.

"You know a lot about wines."

"I've been known to pop a few corks in my day." He lifted an eyebrow.

Her eyes softened. Bobby smiled and

took a generous sip of wine.

CHAPTER 14

Ten minutes before departure, Paul's cell-phone twittered.

"Hey, Paul, glad I caught you before you were in the air. Listen, I won't be in the office today, but Bernie's here and I brought him up to speed—"

Blah, blah, blah, yaddah, yaddah, yaddah, thought Paul as he listened to his investment counselor. He considered canceling, calling Kiri to tell her he was coming home, asking if she needed anything from the store—organic coffee.

"Shit," he muttered. He had an obligation to his mother, whom he hadn't seen in five months. She would surely be looking forward to his visit, and undoubtedly had plans for them.

As he boarded the flight, an attendant smiled just like Cassandra. "Welcome aboard flight...."

***

Bobby drained the rest of the bottle into Kiri's glass and leaned back. His long legs wiggled with nervous energy as she told him about the mysterious mural on her bedroom ceiling. "I gotta see that," he said, noticing that her nipples showed clearly through the T-shirt.

"Sure, anytime you want." She listened to her heart as it swooshed between her ears, reminding her what her sister Yoshi had said about her black experience, 'Oh my god, I've never felt so...occupied.'

"I have something I'd like to share with you." Bobby grasped her hand and led her up the stairs to his bedroom, draining his glass as they went. "This is my baby," he explained, gesturing to a wall rack that displayed a golden bat. "I won the batting title in '96—last day of the season, three-two count, broken bat single. Can you beat that?"

On another wall was the broken bat. He gripped the cracked handle in his hands and took his batting stance.

"This's the bat I did it with—a slider, up and in, laid a nice little blooper just over the glove of the shortstop." He reached up to demonstrate.

Kiri couldn't make sense of it, yet was determined to attend a Binghamton Mets game in the near future. She smiled, grasped the bat, and took an awkward stance.

"Let me show you." Bobby stepped in close from behind to guide her hands. Then he placed a hand on her thigh to adjust her legs. "Just imagine, a fastball comin' ninety-three miles an hour." He moved her arms slowly through the motion of a swing. "You don't blink, you keep your eyes focused on the ball." He pressed against her. "You meet the ball with the fat part of the bat and... wham."

She followed his directions as he took her through the motion over and over. She felt his hardness pressing into her back. He moved her long black hair away from her neck.

"You think I would be a good baseball player?" she asked in a quavering voice.

"Oh yeah," he whispered into her ear, "I know you could handle a bat like a pro." Then he kissed her neck.

Kiri sighed and tilted her head back.

"You wanna know what my number was in the Bigs?"

"What?" She managed as he brushed his

lips against her face.

"Number nine." He pushed his erection against her.

She turned into his arms and he kissed her — soft pillows of flesh, tongues waltzing. Lifting her T-shirt, he gathered a nipple into his mouth and the heat between her legs was nearly unbearable.

"I've never —" Kiri's voice quavered.

Bobby smothered the rest of her sentence with his mouth and backed her toward the king-sized bed. He undressed her and then stepped back to lower his warm-ups. Kiri stared in amazement.

"Relax baby, you with ol' number nine."

CHAPTER 15

Paul's mother had forgotten he was coming.

"I'm going to the Pederson's. You should come too," she encouraged. "It'll be fun — they're always asking about you."

Get-togethers, she called them. He'd grown up with get-togethers. When he was a child he used to sneak near the bottom of the stairs to listen to the slurred cocktail conversations and shallow discourses on popular subjects — politics, sex, sit-coms.

"I'll pass, Mom."

"You sure, dear? Everyone would love to see you."

"Yeah, I'll just vegetate...*kick it,* as the kids say."

"Too bad Kiri couldn't make it...she's like a little China-doll."

"Japanese, Mom; she's Japanese."

"Well, all right then, sweetheart. I'll try to be back early." She hurried out the door as if she were late for bingo.

"Fifty-seven channels and there's nothin' on." He sang Springsteen's ode to television as he surfed. Loneliness wrapped unfeeling arms around him. The house was haunted with memories. As an only child, he remembered the once a year vacations to places he detested, towed along by his parents like wheeled luggage.

He looked at his watch and dialed Kiri, but she didn't answer. He didn't feel like leaving a message. He decided to catch a late afternoon flight and left his mother an apologetic contrivance regarding a sudden business emergency. He would surprise his wife — maybe take her to see the travel agent. They both needed a break from dabbling. A nice vacation, he mused, to make Kiri forget her nonsense. Then they would smother the fucking mural beneath six inches of plaster. He made a plane reservation from his laptop.

***

Bobby traded nipples until Kiri was writhing beneath him. He sat up and lifted her legs by the ankles. She felt the ridge of his helmet slipping past her lips, followed slowly by the broad, luxuriant length of his dark shaft.

"Oh, baby, yeah," he groaned. "Snug as a bug in a rug." He sucked her toes and licked her calves as he pushed down, down, in, in.

Kiri took a deep breath and let out a staccato groan that resonated with the deepest satisfaction.

***

Reluctantly, Kiri returned to her house for a Skype meeting with her father. Bobby Thornton stood naked with the busted bat in his hands, his batting title earned with it.

"Second place gets you nowhere," he reminded himself. "Second place ain't shit." He gazed at the dinner plate-sized wet spot on the comforter. He thought to leave it there for a while as another reminder. "Gotta tap that ass whenever you can." He smiled at his nakedness in the mirror. "Tonight," he pointed to his penis, "ol' number nine's got another date with that tight little sushi-girl."

He thought to call his children—hadn't heard from them in quite a long while. After the divorce, they had grown up mostly without him. His thoughts turned dark. Bitch married a honky, kids had Christmas, Thanksgiving, and the Fourth—

every goddamn holiday with that cracker's family. Bitch traded ol' number nine for a shrimp-dick architect.

"Muthufuckuh." He twisted the bat in his hands until it broke off at the handle. "Muthufuckuh!"

***

Kiri looked at the clock. Paul would be calling anytime, she sighed. She sat in the bathroom and lifted a leg to examine. She had taken a long shower to freshen up. His glowing effluent had seeped endlessly, and now and then she still felt a trickle. Spontaneously she fetched Pandora's Box and tossed it into the backyard trashcan. A crow resting in the top branches of an elm laughed at her. Real pleasure didn't come in a box, she realized, it was found with number nine. And so what if she got pregnant. The possibility made it even more exciting. She would tell her husband that his favorite baseball player donated.

Kiri slipped into a short black mini with a purple silk blouse and stood on black spiked heels. She checked herself one more time in the mirror, descended to the living room to Skype with her father, and when they finished, she put on some blues.

If Father knew about Bobby he would spit, call me a whore and disown me. She remembered how he punished she and Yoshi for being women—no sons for him to teach the mysteries of manhood to. As children, they were treated little better than the chattel. Father decided what they would study at the university to help further his private little empire.

Paul had represented a chance for escape, and when he asked her to marry him four months after they met she didn't hesitate. It had been good for a while. A shadow appeared through the stained glass of the front door. Her dark prince had arrived. She smiled, thinking that she would definitely get Paul out of town more often.

CHAPTER 16

"Thanks for flying..." The flight attendant's practiced shtick was accompanied by the standard faux smile. Paul left the terminal and walked briskly to the airport parking lot to fetch his Jeep.

"Flowers first," he reminded himself, "and then I'll fill her so full of cum at least one tadpole is bound to find the pond." His penis inflated with the thought. One way or another they would have a child and everything would fall into place. He would watch her change into a mother, and as her maternal instincts swelled, he would be on top of the world again.

***

"So it's come to this," grunted Mrs. Gorman, rocking steadily on the porch as late evening sun sifted through the bare winter trees. "Sitting and speculating about the lives of others."

She had watched the good-looking black man from across the street cross the street to the O'Neil house, and he wasn't dressed for a picnic, she noticed. She remembered him visiting Letty Simmons quite often when the rest of her family were out. "Mind your business, old woman," she reprimanded herself. The rocking chair croaked and the floorboards creaked. A sudden rush of sadness filled her eyes, and she looked up into the twilight sky to keep tears from spilling.

She stuffed her hands deeper into the pockets of her heavy coat. For a moment there were no cars, no people, no wind, and when a crow cawed from a skeletal tree, a shiver ran down her spine. "Who will even miss me? Will anybody even notice that I'm gone?"

***

Paul parked on the curb instead of pulling into the carriage house. He wanted to surprise Kiri. It was still early. She would be reading, surfing the Internet, or watching one of those foreign films he never cared for. He would take her out for a nightcap or a late dinner, and somewhere in the course of their conversation they would talk seriously about babies.

He saw Mrs. Gorman rocking alone in the gathering darkness and felt guilty. He left his overnight bag on the seat and walked over. "Hi Mrs. Gorman, how are you?"

"Still rockin'," she joked. "Listen, young man, you're just in time, I baked an apple pie, and I'll wager it's still warm."

"No thanks," he smiled. "You sound like you have a cold," he added.

"Allergies," she lied, blowing into the paper napkin she kept in her coat pocket.

"I'll take a rain check on the pie. Goodnight," he waved, and walked away.

"Okay," she nodded, and then to herself she whispered, "goodnight."

Paul saw that Kiri's Lexus was in the carriage house. He grabbed his bag and the flowers and sneaked into the house, hoping to place them without notice. The downstairs looked empty. He removed his shoes and tiptoed to the staircase. Muffled noises came from the bedroom, and he stood at the edge of the banister to listen. Slowly he made his way up the stairs, avoiding the boards that he knew to creak loudest. He stood outside the bedroom door and heard Kiri's voice, soaring with passion.

The goddamn Pandora's Box, my goddamn

replacement, he thought—an attaché crammed with options. She was frenzied, using sailor language. First chance he got that thing was headed for the dumpster.

"Fuck me, baby, harder, yeah!"

Paul leaned against the hallway wall and sat down. The flowers seemed ridiculous in his hand. He gazed at the second bedroom—the baby room.

"Oh god, I'm cumming…ayyy!" she announced.

Paul determined to replace the bedroom ceiling if need be, just to be rid of Espinoza's paint-by-numbers porno.

"I'm right behind you baby, ohhh shit, awww!" Bobby Thornton growled. Paul's eyes widened and the catch in his throat almost choked him.

"Ayyy!" his wife screamed as the bedsprings busied themselves keeping up with the sudden rush of movement. Paul stood on wobbly legs, chest pounding. He felt dizzy for a moment and sat again.

"Hyyy! Oh baby, oh my god, I'm gonna cum again!" his wife chanted.

Hot, angry tears fell from Paul's eyes, and his lungs couldn't gather enough oxygen. His fingers clawed through his hair to keep sanity from seeping out of his skull.

***

A loud pop shifted Bobby's focus away from seeing his spunk flow out of Kiri. "What the fuck?" he lifted up.

"It was just a backfire baby, get back down here," she begged, reaching for his cock and pulling him down.

***

Mrs. Gorman's apple pie was sitting on the dining room table. An old phonograph was playing Eddie Fisher's, "*I'm Yours.*"

"Mrs. Gorman?" Paul smelled something odd.

He rushed up the stairs, and the door to the Espinoza gallery was open. Smoke drifted in the air and her body was still twitching on the floor, one leg kicking as if it were somehow connected to the music downstairs.

***

Bobby ignored Kiri's pleas and got up to peek through the blinds.

"Ah shit." He hurried back to the bed to gather his clothes.

"What's wrong, baby?" Kiri sat up.

He stepped into his pants and slipped on his shirt. "Your husband is home," he whispered.

"Paul's not due back until tomorrow evening," she tried to soothe him as he forced his shoes on while they were still tied. "Come back to bed."

Without answering, he pecked her on the lips, peeked through the bedroom door, and used the handrails to vault three steps at a time, praying that Paul wasn't waiting with a shotgun.

As Kiri walked to the window, semen dripped to the wooden floor. She opened the blinds with a finger and saw the Jeep parked at the curb.

"Oh, no, no, no." She forced herself to think—wet spots on the top-sheet, cum everywhere. She found her underwear on the bed, wiped the semen off the floor, and tore the bottom sheet off. Then she diapered herself with the underwear and rushed into the bathroom.

If Father ever found out, he would loan me a samurai sword from his collection, she thought as she stepped into the shower. Downstairs, Vivaldi's *Four Seasons* began to play.

***

Paul stood beneath the mural for a moment and then lifted the crumpled bottom sheet to his nose. He looked up at Espinoza. One eye expressed very little and the other said it all.

***

"Ouch." The soap stung as she lathered her dark triangle. Her heart was still pounding when she saw a shadowy silhouette standing on the other side of the privacy glass. She feigned astonishment as she slid the shower door open a crack.

"Paul! You nearly scared me to death, darling! What are you doing home?"

"I brought flowers," he said tersely. "They need water."

***

Bobby knew the drill. He remembered when he was having Letty Simmons on the dining room table when her husband pulled up. He had slinked out the back door, through the side gate, and calmly strolled to the mailbox to check his slot before crossing the street. By the time he saw Paul leaving the old lady's house, he was already standing on his balcony.

"We gonna be all right," he murmured. "Be just fine." He shook his head and smiled. "That crazy girl's got herself a bad case of jungle fever."

He returned to the bedroom, stepped out of his clothes and into the bathroom. He lifted his heavy penis, still glazed with Kiri's juices. "Mm-mm-mm."

Bobby heard a loud pop, followed shortly thereafter by another. He hurried to the balcony window.

"Backfire my ass," he muttered. "Shit, this's gonna be bad." He picked up the phone, set it down, then picked it up again. A few neighbors gathered outside and Bobby put the phone down.

"Sit tight, ride it out," he advised himself. He tapped a button on the CD player, and

Soulja Boy filled the room with various epitaphs.

He stepped into the shower to rinse as a siren wailed in the distance.

"No more married bitches, no sir, not for Bobby Lee Thornton, not ol' number nine."

Author Biography

Ty Spencer Vossler, MFA, is the Xman (ex-farmer, ex-truck driver, ex-powerlifter, ex-cop, expatriate). He currently lives in Tlaxcala, Mexico, with his BMW (beautiful Mexican wife) and daughter. He has taught English and creative writing for twenty-three years, and currently is a professor for the *Colegio ADA* in Puebla, Mexico. His rich life experience has shaped his writings into a reflection of contemporary society. Vossler's published short stories, essays, and poetry have won worldwide acclaim. He attributes his original and creative work to the fact that he shot his television over two decades ago. To learn more about Vossler, visit: www.tyvossler.com.